ONE THREE NINE INSPIRED

XANDER'S
CEREBRAL PALSY
SUPERPOWERS

BOOK 3

WRITTEN BY LORI LEIGH YARBOROUGH, PT

ILLUSTRATED BY ROKSANA OSLIZLO

Published by One Three Nine Inspired Press
Dallas, Texas, U.S.A.

For permissions contact:
superkids@onethreenineinspired.com

Library of Congress Control Number: 2020904604
Library of Congress Cataloging-in-Publication Data
Yarborough, Lori

Xander's Cerebral Palsy Superpowers/ by Lori Leigh Yarborough; illustrated by Roksana Oslizlo

Summary: The superhero of this book, Xander, explains his Cerebral Palsy superpowers,
how they affect him, why he's a valuable member of his family, and that what he's capable of matters.

ISBN-13: 978-1-7326381-5-0 (softcover)

Special thanks to Anita for sharing her stories and pictures of Xander.

Additional thanks to my amazing editor, Lori Freeland, for her patience and dedication.

Disclaimer: This book details the author and child's personal experiences and opinions about
Cerebral Palsy. All other characters are purely fictional. Any similarities to any person are purely
coincidental. The ideas and suggestions in this book are not intended to diagnose, treat, cure, or
prevent any condition. Please consult with your physician, healthcare provider, or specialist
regarding the suggestions and recommendations in this book.

To Xander –
You are an incredible, amazing,
and wonderfully-made hero.
-L.L.Y.

My superpowers come from . . .

CEREBRAL PALSY

Cerebral palsy sounds like—seh-ree-brel pawl-zee

You got it!

Sometimes we shorten it to "CP." It's easier to say.

I don't really have a red suit of armor that lets me fly. But my mom says I am *that awesome* with all my equipment. And I think my dog, Oreo, agrees.

Most people have *no idea* that cerebral palsy comes with superpowers. That's why I want to tell you all about mine.

But first, let's start with why I have CP.

Right before—or maybe while or even after—I was born, the part of my brain that was supposed to control my motor skills got hurt. Motor skills are what we use to walk, talk, sit, and move around.

Basically, my body doesn't do what I want it to do.

CEREBRAL   PALSY

means having to do with the brain

means difficulty moving

Did you know that CP doesn't look the same in every kid? It could be so mild you might not even notice someone has it or so severe someone might have to use a walker or a wheelchair.

There are four kinds of cerebral palsy. Each affects a different part of the body.

SPASTIC

muscles are tight or stiff

ATHETOID OR DYSKINETIC

hard to control movement

ATAXIC

poor balance and coordination

MIXED

a combo of two or more types.

I made a handy, dandy body chart to show you *which kinds* of CP affect *what body parts.*

Look for the colored-in areas on this figure.

Most kids with CP have . . .

MONOPLEGIA HEMIPLEGIA DIPLEGIA QUADRIPLEGIA

SPASTIC CEREBRAL PALSY

That's what I have. Spastic (SPASS – tik) means my muscles feel tight or stiff.

Feel how relaxed your arms or legs can get when you want them to. Mine can't do that. This makes it difficult to do things like move around, play, eat, walk, and talk.

Because sometimes my brain can't tell my muscles what to do, guess what happens? You're right. *They don't do what I want them to do!*

But I've been working hard in therapy, and now I don't use my wheelchair or walker as much as I used to. I can even take Oreo for walks!

My friend, Emmie, has . . .

DYSKINETIC CEREBRAL PALSY

Dyskinetic (dis-ki-ne-tic) or Athetoid cerebral palsy makes her head, arms and legs move in ways she can't control. Her muscles can be really stiff or really loose.

Most of the time, she has to use a wheelchair. Talking isn't easy, but she has this cool device that speaks for her.

You know what else? Emmie loves to ride horses, swim, and play wheelchair sports. She goes to school in a classroom with other kids and is doing great! Friends help her on the playground during recess and include her when they're playing.

Emmie is *smart*, and she *knows* what's going on around her. She's a real superhero.

My buddy, Conner, has . . .

ATAXIC CEREBRAL PALSY

Ataxic (ay-TAK-sik) CP gives him problems with *balance* and *coordination*. He trips and falls a lot. He also has trouble talking.

When Conner was little, he couldn't walk. But he's a *fighter* and one of the most determined kids I know.

And today, Conner can *walk* down the hall using the wall to keep him steady. He *loves life* and always wears a *smile.*

Back to me and Oreo and my . . .

TELEPATHY

—the power of choice for today's superhero.

When mere mortals want to communicate, their brains send signals, and *they say what they want to say.* When I want to communicate, my brain sends signals—only my mouth doesn't get the message.

That's okay.

I can tell you what I want telepathically. Close your eyes. Annnd . . . wait for it. Did you get my message?

Fine. Telepathy isn't actually a *real* superpower. It sounds cool though, so I'm going with it.

SOME TYPES OF COMMUNICATION

Uses words well.

Uses a few words.

Uses sign language.

Not all kids with CP use telepathy like me. Other kids might use talking devices, sign language, words, or a combination of ways to communicate.

Uses a "talker."

Uses "telepathy."
(movements,
gestures, noises,
facial expressions, etc.)

HELPFUL HINTS FOR FRIENDS

If your friend tries to get your attention, see if you can figure out what she needs. It's probably something in the room or something she likes to do. It can be frustrating at first but be patient. The more you get to know her, the better you'll understand her.

Always assume your friend knows what's going on around her. Sometimes she won't respond. Other times she'll use noises, laughter, and movements to show you what she wants.

A superpower that gets me through the day is my . . .

PERSISTENT POSITIVE ATTITUDE

Cerebral palsy might mess with my body, but it can't mess with me. Not much gets me down.

In the middle of everything I have to conquer, my super strength, courage, determination, and bravery keep me *positive.*

HELPFUL HINTS FOR FRIENDS

Your friend has value, worth, and purpose. Just like everyone else, he has good days and bad days. Tell him you believe in him and you're proud of him. Share what you admire about him. Treat him like an equal. Most of all, be kind.

My greatest superpower is . . .

DEDICATED DETERMINATION

My body fights me *all the time!* Things most people do without thinking are extra challenging for me—like putting on my shoes or using my "talker" for communication.

That doesn't mean I'm weak. Nope. I'm *super strong.* To do everyday things, I have to work hard. But that's okay. I just pull out my superhero equipment and get stuff done.

HELPFUL HINTS FOR FRIENDS

It can be difficult for your friend to do something that's easy for you. Cheer him on! He's a superhero. Make sure he knows it. It's great for your friend to learn new skills, but sometimes it's also nice to lend a helping hand.

A perk of my superhero gig is . . .

HIGH TECH SUPERHERO EQUIPMENT

Are you looking for *the coolest* stuff? Not only do I own it, I use it every single day.

Check out my special school bus. There's an elevator outside and a place for my wheelchair inside.

I make this bus look good.

I also have a stander, a special swing,
a wheelchair, a walker, a bike trailer,
and a special trike with safety straps.

Because of my incredible superpowers, I have my own . . .

SPECIAL FORCES TEAM

My mom calls them my therapy team. We train together every week.

My *physical therapist* is in charge of my whole-body superpowers like strengthening, stretching, and walking. She also makes sure my equipment fits.

My *occupational therapist* works on fine-tuning my finger movements, my hand skills, sensory integration stuff, and eating strategies. Basically, we do things that help me with everyday activities.

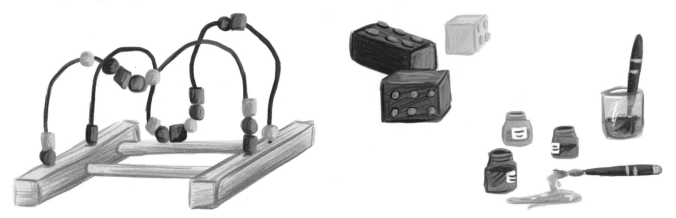

My *speech pathologist* is my communication commando. She helps with any talking issues I have and figures out the best way for me to let others know what I want or need.

My Special Forces Team helps me *harness my superpowers.* These awesome people love me, teach me new skills, and always cheer me on. They get very excited when I try new things.

HELPFUL HINTS FOR FRIENDS

Therapy is tough. But keeping my muscles stretched and strong and working on balance is so important. Hand skills and sensory activities can be exhausting. Learning new ways to communicate can be frustrating. Find ways to encourage your friend not to give up. Maybe you can even do activities and exercises with him.

I have a special assistant at school. She's my . . .

SUPERHERO SIDEKICK

Batman had Robin. The Lone Ranger had Tonto. And I have Kelly.

That sounds cool *because she is cool.* She helps me get around school and makes sure I'm where I'm supposed to be.

Every great superhero has a nemesis. Mine is my . . .

SUPER SELECTIVE MUSCULAR STRENGTH

My body resists me. Sometimes it makes sudden movements I wasn't planning on. That can seem scary to other people. I might want to put my hand on the table gently. But instead, my brain sends a signal to hit the table really hard.

The muscles that make that movement are really strong, and I can't always control them.

So if you see me move unexpectedly, don't worry. It's just my Super Selective Muscular Strength taking over.

HELPFUL HINTS FOR FRIENDS

If your friend gets excited or scared, you can help him by making sure he stays safe. Watch that he doesn't hit his head on something or fall. If your friend is tired or stressed, his arms and legs won't want to listen to what his brain wants them to do. When he slaps the table or kicks something, he might look alarmed or upset. Don't worry. Just be calm and get an adult if you feel like something is wrong.

We interrupt this broadcast . . . I mean book . . . to bring you—

QUESTIONS & ANSWERS

You have questions? I have answers. Oreo's just here for support

WHY DOES YOUR ARM MOVE THAT WAY?

My arm can get really stiff. Especially if I'm tired or stressed.

CAN I ASK YOU QUESTIONS ABOUT YOUR WHEELCHAIR?

Yes! My mom or I would be happy to tell you all about my ride.

WHY DO YOU USE A WHEELCHAIR WHEN YOU CAN WALK?

It takes tons of energy to walk. It can even hurt. A lot. I use my wheelchair when I'm worn out or need to go longer distances.

WHY DO YOU WALK DIFFERENTLY THAN ME?

Sometimes my muscles make it hard to walk. And when I'm tired, my legs don't listen very well to my brain.

WHAT ARE YOU WEARING ON YOUR FEET?

AFOs. Ankle-Foot Orthotics. They help me stand and walk.

DO YOU WANT TO HANG OUT WITH ME ON THE PLAYGROUND?

Absolutely! I love hanging out with friends. Especially if we play things I can do. If I'm in my wheelchair, offer to push me where we're going. If I'm walking, wait up for me. A good friend doesn't leave anyone behind.

WITH XANDER & OREO

HOW DO I TALK TO AND HANG OUT WITH KIDS WITH CEREBRAL PALSY?

Smile and say,

"Hi! My name is _____. You wanna hang out?"

Most kids with cerebral palsy understand as much as you do even if they can't speak. Talk about things you like—your dog, family, sports teams.

Don't worry if someone has a hard time talking or can't talk at all. Smile and treat kids with CP like any other friend.

Don't lean or hang on their wheelchair or walker. Don't be nervous.

Do smile, stay calm, and have fun.

As an important and valuable part of my family, I like to be . . .

WHERE MY PEOPLE ARE

I go where my family goes. If they go on an adventure, I go on an adventure. We love to swim in our pool, bike in the park, and play at the beach.

My brothers and sisters think I'm fun to hang with.

My dad calls me his *X-man.* We like to laugh together.

My mom says I'm kind and compassionate. When someone in my family is sad, I'm ready to help.

And by the way, Oreo and I are always up for ice cream dates!

YOUR SUPERPOWERS

All kids have superpowers. You probably have some of the
same superpowers as me and some that are unique to you.
Write down your name and Superpowers below.

_____'S SUPERPOWERS

YOU ARE IMPORTANT

You are UNIQUELY you

You're a **FIGHTER**

You have **SO MUCH** value and **SO MUCH** worth

YOU'RE INCREDIBLE

THE WORLD NEEDS YOU

The things **YOU** can do **MATTER**

I want to fit in just like every other kid. I love to watch movies, play games, and have fun with family and friends.

There is no one else like me. I have value and worth and an important place in this world.

And superpowers.

Don't forget my superpowers.

MEET XANDER!

Xander was adopted from Ukraine. He now lives in his forever home in Oklahoma with his mom, dad, three sisters, two brothers, and three dogs—Oreo, Sadie and Louie.

He loves tight hugs, holding hands, and swaying to music.

AVAILABLE ON AMAZON.COM

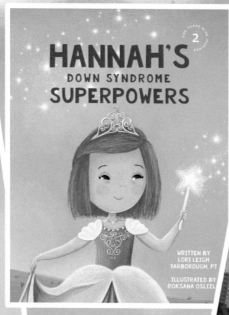

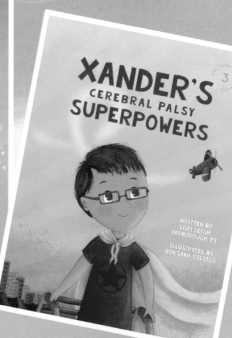

FIND US AT:

139 Inspired Kids Books

Each 139 Inspired book is written about a specific child in corroboration with his or her parents. The information given is about that particular child's superpowers but will be relatable to other children with the same diagnosis and abilities.

This book is an *EDUCATIONAL ADVOCATE TOOL* to help children and their friends, families, and caregivers understand kids with superpowers. Understanding promotes *compassion and empathy* which promotes *inclusion and friendship.*

All children need to know they're wanted, loved, and special. All children need to know they have superpowers. And all children especially need to know they're wonderfully made.

"I WILL PRAISE YOU, BECAUSE I AM
FEARFULLY AND WONDERFULLY MADE;
YOUR WORKS ARE WONDERFUL.
I KNOW THAT FULL WELL."

PSALMS 139:14

The inspirational art on the next page has been designed especially for you. Cut it out, decide which side you like best, and hang it up.

I AM FEARFULLY AND WONDERFULLY MADE

I AM FEARFULLY AND WONDERFULLY MADE

Made in the USA
Monee, IL
13 October 2021

The superhero of this book, Xander, explains his Cerebral Palsy superpowers, how they affect him, why he's a valuable member of his family, and that what he's capable of matters.

LORI LEIGH YARBOROUGH is a physical therapist and graduate of the University of Oklahoma Health Sciences Center. She lives with her husband and four children in Texas. When her son was diagnosed on the Autism Spectrum, she came up with the idea of "superpowers" to explain to him why he interacted with the world the way he did. The One Three Nine Inspired Series was created to show all kids they're wonderfully made.

ISBN 978-1-7326381-5-0   US$12.95

51295>

9 781732 638150

HOCKEY

Stats, Facts, and Figures

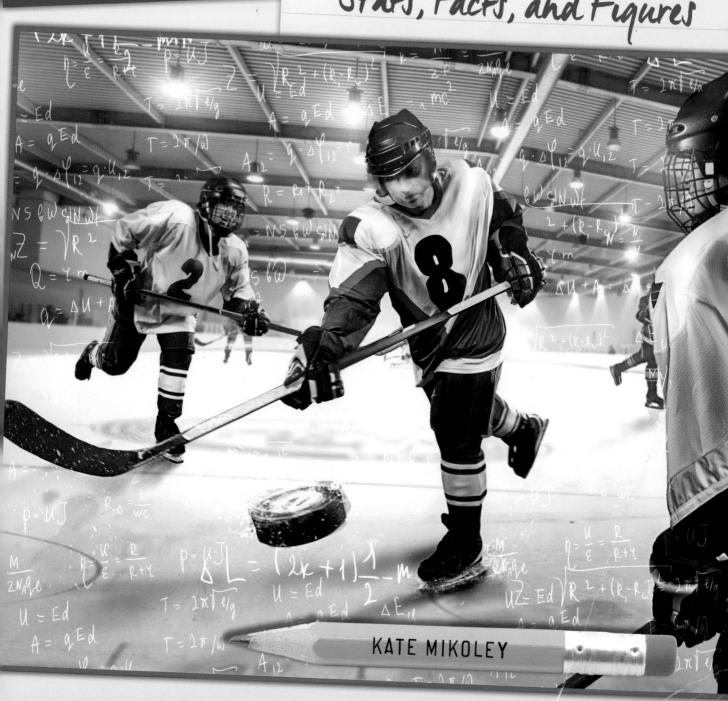

KATE MIKOLEY